Franklin and the Cookies

From an episode of the animated TV series *Franklin*, produced by Nelvana Limited, Neurones France s.a.r.l. and Neurones Luxembourg S.A, based on the Franklin books by Paulette Bourgeois and Brenda Clark.

Story written by Sharon Jennings.

Illustrated by Céleste Gagnon, John Lei, Sasha McIntyre and Shelley Southern.

Based on the TV episode *Franklin's Cookie Question*, written by Bruce Robb.

 ™ Kids Can Read is a trademark of Kids Can Press Ltd.

Franklin

Franklin is a trademark of Kids Can Press Ltd.
The character of Franklin was created by Paulette Bourgeois and Brenda Clark.
Text © 2005 Contextx Inc.
Illustrations © 2005 Brenda Clark Illustrator Inc.

Kids Can Press acknowledges the financial support of the Government of Ontario, through the Ontario Media Development Corporation's Ontario Book Initiative; the Ontario Arts Council; the Canada Council for the Arts; and the Government of Canada, through the BPIDP, for our publishing activity.

Published in Canada by
Kids Can Press Ltd.
29 Birch Avenue
Toronto, ON M4V 1E2

Published in the U.S. by
Kids Can Press Ltd.
2250 Military Road
Tonawanda, NY 14150

www.kidscanpress.com

Series editor: Tara Walker
Edited by Jennifer Stokes
Designed by Céleste Gagnon

Printed and bound in China by WKT Company Limited

CM 05 0 9 8 7 6 5 4 3 2 1
CM PA 05 0 9 8 7 6 5 4 3 2 1

National Library of Canada Cataloguing in Publication Data

Jennings, Sharon
    Franklin and the cookies / Sharon Jennings ;
illustrated by Céleste Gagnon ... [et al.].

(Kids Can read)
The character Franklin was created by Paulette Bourgeois and Brenda Clark.

ISBN 1-55337-716-8 (bound).   ISBN 1-55337-717-6 (pbk.)

I. Gagnon, Céleste II. Bourgeois, Paulette III. Clark, Brenda IV. Title. V. Series: Kids Can read (Toronto, Ont.)

PS8569.E563F7156 2005   jC813'.54   C2004-903315-8

Kids Can Press is a ℓ☺∩ς™ Entertainment company

Franklin and the Cookies

Kids Can Press

Franklin can tie his shoes.

Franklin can count by twos.

And Franklin can make

really good cookies.

Sometimes this is a problem.

Sometimes Franklin's cookies are *too* good.

One day, Franklin and Bear

were playing tag.

"Whew!" said Bear. "I'm hungry."

"Me too" said Franklin.

"Let's go to my house and make cookies."

"Good idea," said Bear.

Franklin and Bear ran into the kitchen.

They got out butter
and eggs.

They got out sugar
and flour.

They got out lots and lots
of chocolate chips.

They measured and stirred
and mixed.

They plopped spoonfuls
of cookie dough
on a cookie tray.

Franklin's mother put the cookie tray
in the oven.

Then Franklin and Bear waited.

And waited.

DING! went the oven timer.

Franklin's mother pulled out the cookie tray.

"How many cookies do I get?" Bear asked.

"We made one dozen," said Franklin.

"That's twelve cookies," said Bear.

"So we each get six."

"Great," said Franklin. "I can eat

lots and lots of cookies!"

Franklin and Bear poured milk and sat down.

"You have a lot of cookies,"

said Franklin's mother.

Franklin shook his head.

"I can *never* have too many cookies," he said.

"Maybe you can share your cookies

with Harriet and Beatrice,"

said Franklin's mother.

"But Harriet and Beatrice aren't here,"

said Franklin.

"They're at their swimming lesson,"

said Franklin's mother.

"And they will be hungry

when they get back."

"Hmph," said Franklin.

"Hmph," said Bear.

Bear looked at his cookies.

"I have six cookies," he said.

"That means I have to give three cookies to Beatrice."

"And I have to give three cookies to Harriet," said Franklin.

Bear made two piles
of three cookies.

So did Franklin.

Bear gobbled up one pile.

So did Franklin.

Franklin and Bear went outside to play.

Soon, Franklin said, "My sister is too little

to eat three cookies."

Bear agreed.

"So is my sister," he said.

"But *I* can *never* have too many cookies,"

said Franklin.

"Me neither," said Bear.

"Hmmm," said Franklin.

"Hmmm," said Bear.

Franklin and Bear ran inside.

They each ate one more cookie.

"Two cookies are

still a lot of cookies,"

said Bear.

"Two cookies are

almost as many

as three cookies,"

said Franklin.

They each ate one more cookie.

"One cookie each doesn't look

like much," said Franklin.

"One cookie is almost like no cookies,"

said Bear.

They ate the last two cookies.

Franklin looked at the cookie plate.

"Uh-oh," he said. "When is

the swimming lesson over?"

"Three o'clock," said Bear.

Franklin looked

at the clock.

It was three o'clock.

"Uh-oh,"

Franklin said again.

But then he had an idea.

Franklin and Bear ran into the kitchen.

They got out butter and eggs.

They got out sugar and flour.

They got out lots and lots
of chocolate chips.

They measured and stirred and mixed.

They plopped spoonfuls of cookie dough

on a cookie tray.

Franklin's father put the cookie tray

in the oven.

Then they waited.

And waited.

DING! went the oven timer.

Franklin's father pulled out

the cookie tray.

"You have a lot of cookies," he said.

"Some are for Harriet and Beatrice,"

said Franklin.

"Good!" said his father. "I'm glad

you want to share."

"Of course," said Franklin.

Franklin and Bear looked at the cookies.

"I still say three cookies

are too many

for my little sister,"

said Bear.

"Harriet could *never*

eat three cookies,"

said Franklin.

Franklin and Bear each ate a cookie.

And so …

… when Harriet and Beatrice got home,

all the cookies were gone.

"Where are our cookies?"

asked Harriet.

But then Franklin

had an idea.

"I'll get my recipe," he said.

"You and Beatrice can help

make the cookies."

Franklin's Cookie Recipe

1	egg	1
125 mL	soft butter	1/2 cup
250 mL	flour	1 cup
250 mL	sugar	1 cup
250 mL	chocolate chips	1 cup

Set the oven to 180°C (350°F).

Beat the egg with the butter.

Mix in the flour and sugar.

Stir in the chocolate chips.

Plop spoonfuls of cookie dough

on a cookie tray.

Ask an adult to put the tray in the oven.

Set the oven timer for 10 minutes.

Let cool, and enjoy.

DING! went the oven timer.

Everyone sat down to eat cookies.

"I'm glad you are sharing

your cookies, Franklin," said his mother.

Franklin smiled.

"Sometimes even *I* can have

too many cookies," he said.